Tucker Gets Tuckered

A book about a dog named Tucker, by two guys named Ted.

Illustrations by Theodore Waddell

Story by Ted Beckstead

This is an Original Flash of Brilliance® Book for Young Readers

Tucker is a dog.

A pretty big dog.

He likes to share his lunch with a friend.

And sometimes eats Kitty's lunch too!

Tucker and his friend Sam also like ice cream.

Sometimes they wait outside
the kitchen for hours
hoping to get just a little taste.

One day after lunch,
Tucker was looking for
someone to play with.

TUCKER HAS AN ENDORSEMENT FROM..... — HE DOES HALF PAIRS, SOMETIMES A GLOVE OR A CLOG.

So Ted took Tucker
and his friends out
for a ride in his truck.

And golfing.

And snorkeling.

And to the botanical garden.

TUCKER SAYS THAT HE DOESN'T LIKE SUMMER, TOO HOT FOR BERNERS, BUT THE OTHER DAY I SAW HIM SMELLING THE ROSES.

And to the beach.

LILLY LIKES THE BEACH. SHE NEEDS SUNBLOCK FOR HER NOSE.

When Tucker got home
he could hardly climb the stairs
he was plum *tuckered* out!

So he fell asleep
on Mimi's lap for a while.

But finally made it up
to bed.

BETTE CALLS GIETEL "THE BUNNY". SHE IS ALWAYS UP.
SHE SLEEPS UNDER THE BED SOMETIMES. SINCE MENOPAUSE SHE IS TOO FAT TO FIT ALL
THE WAY UNDER IT. SO SHE STICKS OUT.

And soon everyone
was sleeping soundly.

GRETEL, TUCKER, LILLY & CHAUNCEY - WHEN HE IS
VISITING ALL SLEEP IN OUR BEDROOM IT'S
LIKE SLEEPING IN A DORM - SNORING GRETEL
IS THE WORST

Tomorrow was another day...

Lilly watches. Sometimes she watches birds. Sometimes she just watches.

To play with friends.

TUCKER IS LEARNING TO PANT. HE WORKS PART TIME AS A TIRE PUMP.

TUCKER BOUNCES DOWNSTAIRS LIKE A SLINKY ON A POGO STICK

Help out in the office.

Lounge around.

And sit on Ted's foot.

That's Tucker!
He's *always* up to something.

Flash of Brilliance ® is a registered trademark of
The Flash of Brilliance Company LLC
PO BOX 45330
Phoenix, Arizona
85064

THANKS STEPH!

ISBN 0-9719515-6-X
Library of Congress Control Number: 2006937227